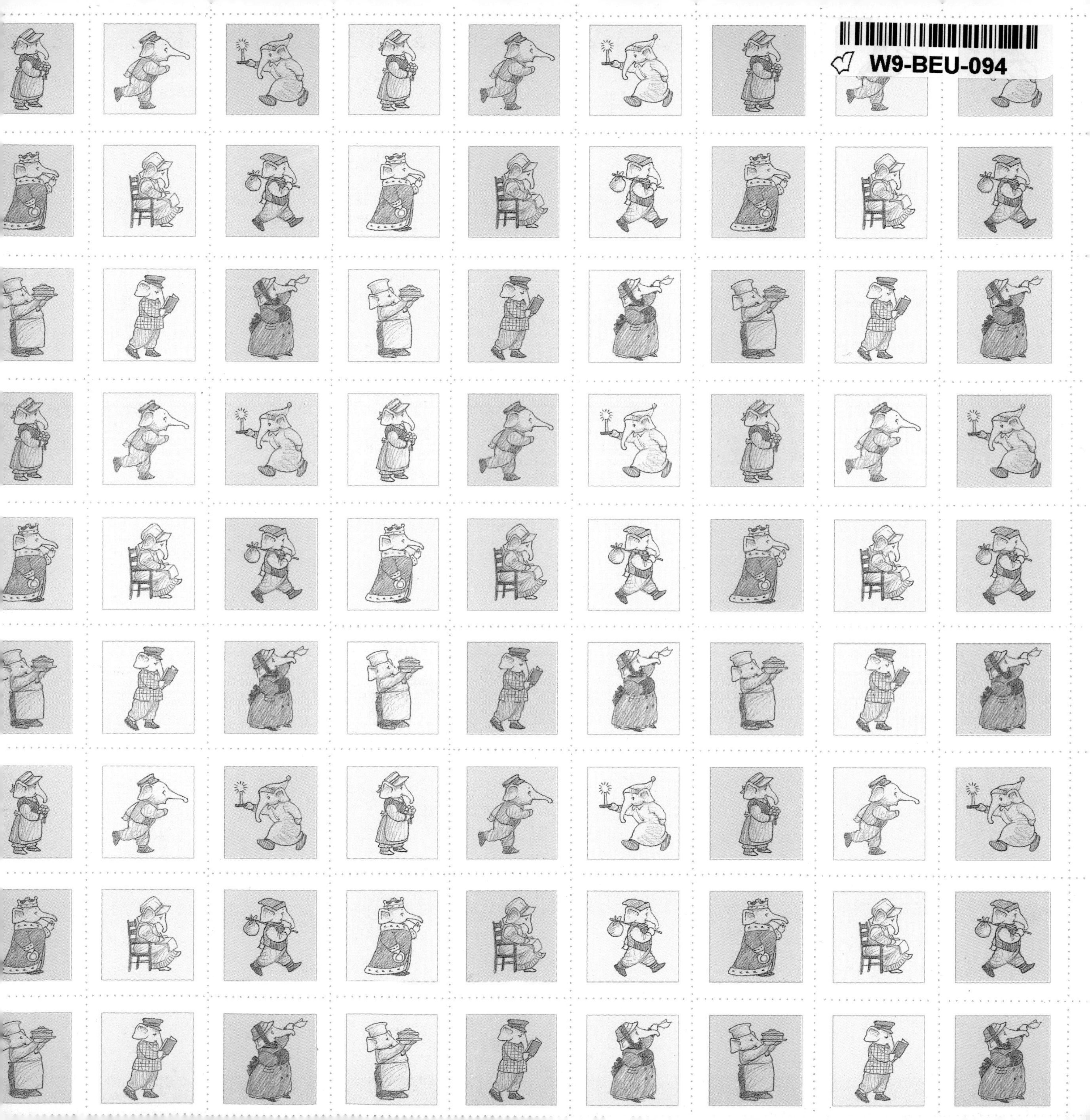

For Juli

Elephants Never Forget

Classic Nursery Rhymes
Illustrated by Graham Percy

CHRONICLE BOOKS • SAN FRANCISCO

CONTENTS

Little Miss Muffet
Sat on a tuffet,
Eating her curds and whey;
There came a big spider,
Who sat down beside her,
And frightened Miss Muffet away.

Simple Simon met a pieman,
Going to the fair;
Says Simple Simon to the pieman,
Let me taste your ware.

Says the pieman to Simple Simon,
Show me first your penny;
Says Simple Simon to the pieman,
Indeed, I have not any.

Little Boy Blue,
Come blow your horn!
The sheep's in the meadow,
The cow's in the corn.

But where is the boy
Who looks after the sheep?
He's under a haystack
Fast asleep!

Will you wake him?
No, not I;
For if I do,
He's sure to cry.

Peter, Peter, pumpkin-eater,
Had a wife and couldn't keep her;
He put her in a pumpkin shell,
And there he kept her very well.

Ring around the rosey
A pocket full of posies
Ashes, ashes,
We all fall down.

The king has sent his daughter,
To fetch a pail of water,
Ashes, ashes,
We all fall down.

The robin on the steeple,
Is singing to the people,
Ashes, ashes,
We all fall down.

Old King Cole
Was a merry old soul,
And a merry old soul was he;
He called for his pipe,
And he called for his bowl,
And he called for his fiddlers three.

Bobby Shafto's gone to sea,
Silver buckles at his knee;
He'll come back and marry me,
Bonny Bobby Shafto!

Bobby Shafto's bright and fair,
Combing down his yellow hair;
He's my love for evermore,
Bonny Bobby Shafto!

One, two,
Buckle my shoe;

Three, four,
Knock at the door;

Five, six,
Pick up sticks;

Seven, eight,
Lay them straight;

Nine, ten,
A big fat hen.

Diddle, diddle, dumpling, my son John,
Went to bed with his stockings on;
One shoe off, and one shoe on;
Diddle, diddle, dumpling, my son John.

Jack be nimble;
Jack be quick;
Jack jump over
The candlestick.

London Bridge is falling down,
Falling down, falling down.
London Bridge is falling down,
My fair lady.

Build it up with wood and clay,
Wood and clay, wood and clay,
Build it up with wood and clay,
My fair lady.

Georgie Porgie, pudding and pie,
Kissed the girls and made them cry;
When the boys came out to play,
Georgie Porgie ran away.

8
6
5
4
3
2
1

To market, to market, to buy a fat pig,
Home again, home again, jiggety-jig;
To market, to market, to buy a fat hog,
Home again, home again, jiggety-jog.

Rub-a-dub-dub,
Three men in a tub;
And who do you think they be?
The butcher, the baker,
The candlestick-maker;
Turn 'em out, knaves all three!

Jack Sprat could eat no fat,
His wife could eat no lean,
And so between them both, you see,
They licked the platter clean.

Mary, Mary, quite contrary,
How does your garden grow?
With silver bells and cockle shells,
And pretty maids all in a row.

Jack and Jill went up the hill
To fetch a pail of water;
Jack fell down and broke his crown
And Jill came tumbling after.

Up Jack got and home did trot
As fast as he could caper;
He went to bed and bound his head
With vinegar and brown paper.

Wee Willie Winkie runs through the town,
Upstairs and downstairs, in his nightgown;
Rapping at the window, crying through the lock,
Are all the children in their beds?
It's past eight o'clock.

First published in Great Britain in 1992 by
Little, Brown and Company, (UK) Limited
Brigade House, 8 Parsons Green, London SW6 4TN
First published in North America in 1992 by Chronicle Books.

Interior design by Lisa Tai
Jacket design by Carry Leeb

ISBN 0-8118-0239-6
CIP Data available.

10 9 8 7 6 5 4 3 2 1

Color separations by Fotographics, Hong Kong
Printed and bound in Italy by Amilcare Pizzi SpA
Distributed in Canada by Raincoast Books,
112 East Third Avenue, Vancouver, B.C. VST IC8

Chronicle Books
275 Fifth Street
San Francisco, California 94103

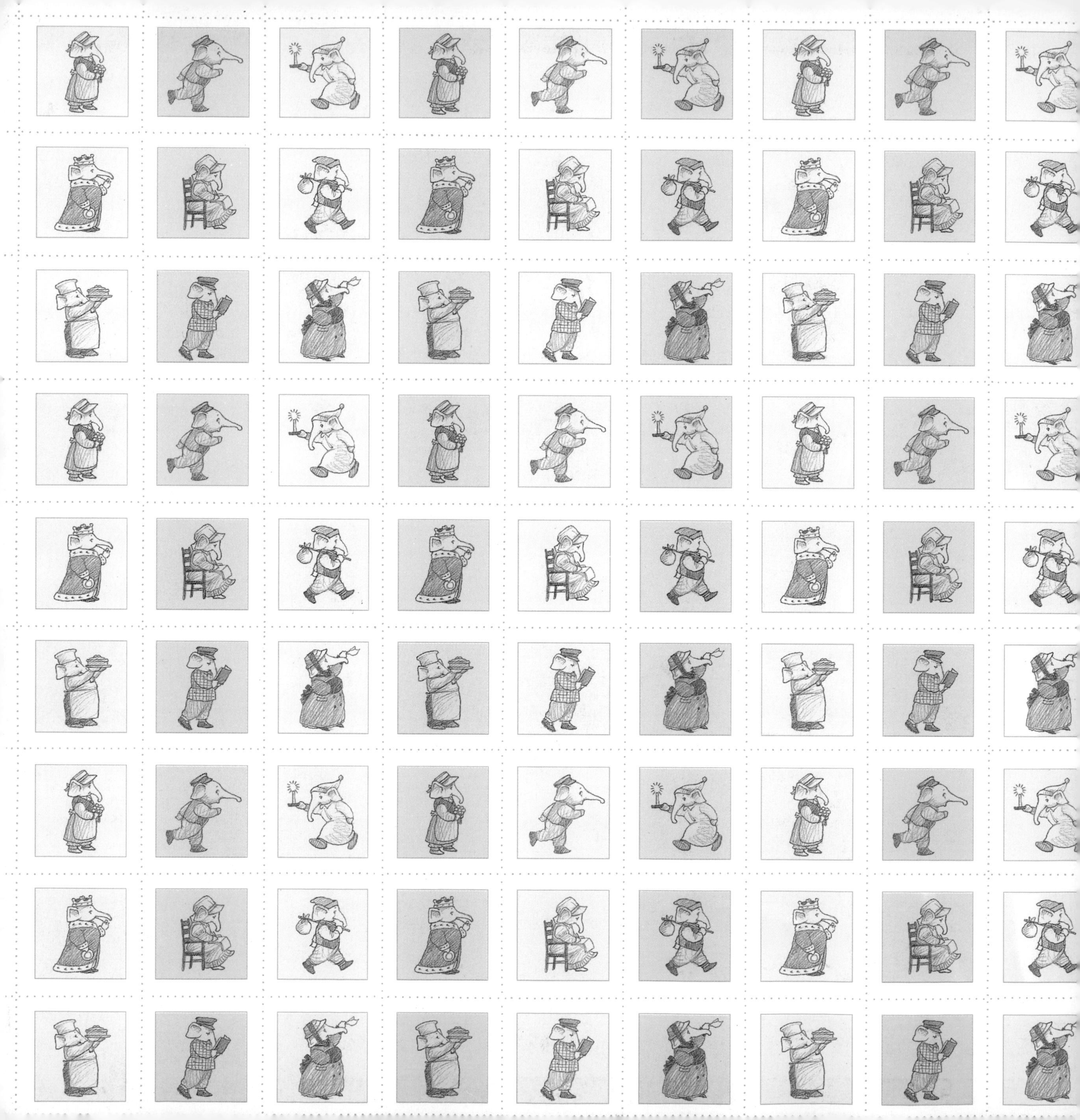